RAVE REVIEWS OF *SITTING IN THE CLUB CAR*.

"If the mind is a galaxy, Paulette Jiles is an astronaut ... nothing is outside her range. Jiles deserves to be a household name ... more fizz and sparkle than a giant bottle of soda." — *Toronto Star*

"Jiles is funny, audacious, witty and crisp."   — *Calgary Herald*

"Jiles writes with rhythmic zest and vivacious elegance."
                                                    — *Ottawa Citizen*

"Jiles won the 1984 Governor-General's Award and she is still defying gravity. Campy and outrageous, sparkling, sassy, she is like a little girl dressing up in her mother's best clothes. There is nothing linear or predictable about Jiles' delivery ... *Sitting in the Club Car* glitters with observation, wit and reflection, beautifully realized at its own fanciful level."
                                                    — *Books in Canada*

"She has remarkable versatility and breadth of interest. *Rum and Karma-Kola* has achieved a kind of cult status."
                                                    — *Bloomsbury Review*

"Paulette Jiles is for this century and for all history. Hers is a force rarely among us — she is a greatness of the first order of magnitude."   — Gordon Lish

ALSO BY PAULETTE JILES

POETRY:
Waterloo Express (Anansi, 1973)
Celestial Navigation (McClelland & Stewart, 1984)
The Jesse James Poems (Polestar, 1988)
Blackwater: New & Selected Poems (Knopf, 1988)

FICTION:
The Late Great Human Road Show (Talonbooks, 1986)
Song To The Rising Sun (Polestar, 1989)
Enemy Women (HarperCollins, 2002)

NON-FICTION:
Cousins (Knopf, 1992)
North Spirit (Doubleday, 1995)

Sitting

IN THE Club Car Drinking Rum AND Karma-Kola

A MANUAL OF ETIQUETTE FOR LADIES
CROSSING CANADA BY TRAIN

PAULETTE JILES

POLESTAR
An Imprint of Raincoast Books

Copyright © 1986 by Paulette Jiles
This edition published in 2003

Polestar and Raincoast Books acknowledge the ongoing financial support of the
Government of Canada through The Canada Council for the Arts and the Book
Publishing Industry Development Program (BPIDP); and the Government of British
Columbia through the BC Arts Council.

Interior design and train illustration: Ingrid Paulson

A portion of the present text appeared in *The Malahat Review*.

*Thanks to Bonnie Evans for the hat and the adventuress kit, and to Rita Moir for keeping my dog
while I went about on trains.*

CANADIAN CATALOGUING IN PUBLICATION DATA

Jiles, Paulette, 1943–
    Sitting in the club car drinking rum & karma-kola
    ISBN 1-55192-640-7
    I. Title. II. Title: A manual of etiquette for ladies crossing Canada by train.
PS8569.I44S5 1986   C813'.54   C86-091488-7
PR9199.3J54S5 1986

LIBRARY OF CONGRESS CONTROL NUMBER: 2003104339

Polestar/Raincoast Books   *In the United States:*
9050 Shaughnessy Street   Publishers Group West
Vancouver, British Columbia   1700 Fourth Street
Canada V6P 6E5   Berkeley, California
www.raincoast.com   94710

Printed in Canada by AGMV Marquis Imprimeur

10 9 8 7 6 5 4 3 2 1

To my mother,
Ruby Lee Jiles

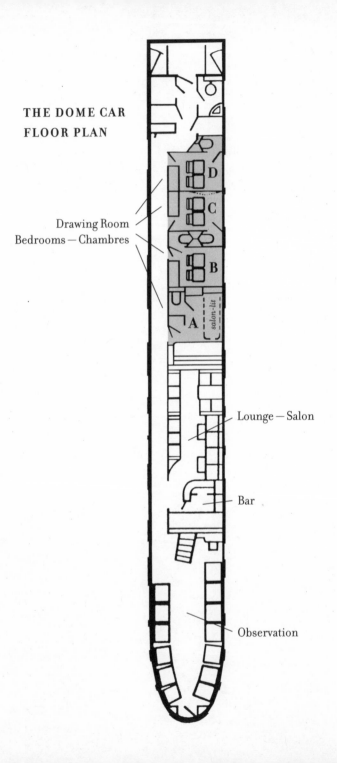

THE DOME CAR FLOOR PLAN

Drawing Room
Bedrooms — Chambres

D

C

B

A   *salon-lit*

Lounge — Salon

Bar

Observation

Opening Scene

S he is entraining for the East somewhere, as Myrna Loy and Jean Arthur and Carole Lombard used to entrain on The Twentieth Century Limited, walking down the concrete apron beside the large cars — minor characters exiting stage left and arriving stage right — with matching luggage and a hat with feathers and a porter reaching for her bags. You've seen it a million times in black and white: steam whistling out from between the teeth of the wheels, very swank and pre-bomb. She's finding it easier to depart and effect closure, to become impermeable, like a trench coat, to *not care* about leaving somebody, to *not care* even if it was her fault (and of course it was her fault); finding it easier to cease something than to start another new thing, to leave America than to escape to Canada.

Through the Gate

A distinguishing characteristic of "hard-boiled" detective fiction is that the heroines, who are always tramps of some utterly enchanting sort, are rescued and forgiven by the hard-boiled one and made pure again, usually by violence and repentance. Violence and repentance: major cultural characteristics of Americans with their Movietone memories, including hers, as she walks through Gate Four struggling with her bags, too confused to find a redcap, and the porters saying, "Car 129? Straight ahead, ma'am."

Foreigners

And now she is almost running, afraid of her misdemeanors back there across the border in America; but she has faith in herself. She has the capacity to invent stories, as long as she has an audience, as long as she has you, the reader, for whom to invent them. They are often outrageous lies, having gone beyond the bounds of "story," but they are engaging and oddly believable.

I'll make my way to Montreal and meet him or somebody there, and everything will work itself out. What life on a Canadian train needs is some vigorous presence, some dash: a few lies, some inventions, a script, a shooter, a storyboard, depth of field; whatever it is, it's starring Katharine Hepburn.

She is almost running, trying to remember that she is in another country; she's in a *province*.

Minor Characters; The Mink Coat

British Columbia, a province, begins on the West Coast with a dinner of rain; then it has a few drinks. If the sea could rise, it would. She is too tall to be of any comfort to short men and she's wearing a navy pin-stripe suit and a pillbox hat with a face veil. Secondhand treasures. She imagines herself in her favourite 1940s movie; love those train scenes.

I've got a secret bank account, astronomical debts, a chariot of fire, and a gift certificate to the treasure of the Sierra Madre. I'm an African Queen and I've got a spare heart that works.

This is the kind of thing you've got to tell yourself after being fired, after a divorce, after walking out on him, after running up an immense amount of credit card debts, after having left Seattle on an impulse, after having gone to Vancouver and bought a series of train tickets on your VISA that will take you across unknown provinces; this is the kind of thing you have to tell yourself. Then you won't get depressed, or desperate; you won't have around you that shiny aura of somebody who doesn't know where her next train ticket is coming from. She is determined to stay cheerful, and anyway she's leaving everybody for a remote city called Montreal. It's raining in West Coast buckets, and as she is helped up the steps the mahogany mink coat goes damp and sulky; it seems to know it hasn't yet been paid for. Mink are creatures of water and earth and don't believe in plastic cash. *Never mind*; she runs behind the porter to her compartment. *Just never, never mind.*

For Lupe Velez

The Vancouver train station is a construction of 1890 dignities and recent decorative blunders. In the park outside there are great architectonic oak trees, and in one corner a catalpa tree hanging all over with green bean pods like syllables, eternally waving its fat round leaves at eternally arriving and departing trains. This tree is for people who have nobody to wave them off; a free service from trees. Now, with the wind, it turns its back on the whole idea and drops catalpa-bean capsules, as if it were a junkie suddenly discovered by police: *open up in there!* The catalpa tree throws up its hands, and the train whistles, and begins to move, and pigeons take off like applause.

The transcontinental moves out of the moist city of Vancouver, leaving behind the city's rainy sea-buses and its steam clock, people in Kerrisdale buying red Princess phones, others in North Vancouver wondering where they left their ironing-board covers, people in the East End always trying to get across Hastings alive; some do. She is not thinking about her debts, or the computers busily filing her several names, about skip-tracers in Canada in pursuit of American cash. She is not thinking about how and when she will go to sleep (it will be somewhere on a train, moving) or how maybe this time the insomnia will evaporate, or how in her dreams the remnants of the imaginations of suicides — like gasoline rags, potentially combustible — will slide down out of the ether just above her dreams. Coming halfway down the stairs of the mind and then going back up again. And then coming back down again. No flames.

For reasons of her own she wants to evoke that era of the forties when daring heroines in mink jackets and pillbox hats got on trains, that safe past before mass extinctions and hidden toxins occupied our mental galaxies. When Amelia Earhart got into an airplane and disappeared forever, when Lauren Bacall went to the Caribbean to buy a hat and departed. That was *To Have and Have Not*. Like most people she confuses real events in the past with events on film; call her Our Heroine.

American Money

American money is narrow and long like Virginia Woolf's feet. It promises a democratic American wealth; freedom from the environment. It says you can leave a poisoned and indebted Earth and live on the moon in a space pickup with a crew cab and shoot pool for high stakes in a dude ranch west somewhere on Mars. American money is all green in all denominations, worn down by free and hungry hands that have extracted the max from every single one-dollar bill; the eye on the pyramid gazing out indifferently on time-travelers. American money is disappearing into electronic devices where it can't say anything anymore with its pyramid eye. Caged, trapped, immobilized in electronic devices, American money evades the single mothers who crash their fists on computers' chassis and say *But I don't owe that much!* And American money says *Oh yes you do, I've got the file right here.* American money disappears down the ratholes of artillery; stuck in the electronic lockup, American dollars are becoming evasive and shy.

She feels she has liberated fifty thousand of the little prisoners, put them back into circulation; they are all working for her and productive. Where to go next? Maybe she'll go and liberate some Honduran dollars, help them with their international debts; or maybe Mexico. She's heard that if you put ten thousand American dollars in a Mexican bank, you could simply live off the grateful interest the Mexican government would present to you. It's a thought, anyway.

Canadian Money

Canadian dollars are blue, green, red, orange, violet and brown. Sometimes all on the same bill. They fold up in her billfold like the colours of exotic confusion. Technicolor money. They display Mounties on horses, carrying lances, pointed inwards in a circle of black animals. They brag about their purple oil refineries, they revere mountain lakes. Blue fishing boats sail off into an azure maritime sea. You are invited to spend them on American products, American movies, American televisions and American books. She will do none of these things. She will take a Canadian train. Happy landings to you, Amelia Earhart.

Unemployment in Heaven

Also getting on the train are a group of Americans, apparently having fallen out of the United States the way minor angels fall out of clouds every time there is unemployment in heaven.

Well, what do they know?

People make observations on her life all the time, as if they were up in the Dome and her life were sliding by outside them, a pictorama, and they were being asked to comment on it. And they could say, "That's a nice mountain," or "I don't find this part of the Great Plain very interesting." She has plans of running away from everything and becoming a charming drunk. But how to go about it? It's expensive!

Charge it.

Changes

The Americans are from Baton Rouge and Houston; they work for airlines and they never want to see another airplane again. They are going to play Clue all the way across Canada. The train is going to simply keep going, the landscape is going to fall into place, the tracks are going to align themselves with absolute precision from here to Halifax, and the brightest proposition of all is the mysterious city at the end of her journey. It's mysterious because she doesn't know which city it's going to be. Call her Our Heroine. And as the porter carries her matching pigskin luggage into Compartment C she glances at the Americans down in the lounge, and decides not to tell them she is an American too, only changed. She wants to be the only American aboard. She came up here to get away from Americans. She liked the thought of "British Columbia," *la Colombie Britannique*. How could anybody resist *a province*, and especially a province with a second French name like that? Both French and western; it's kind of swank, really. The porter did not tell her he, too, was changed; only French.

Falling in Love With Hats

The VIA Rail transcontinental has a blunt blue-and-yellow head on it that will drive through sheer mountain walls and extend its long neck into the stretches of the East, carrying her with it, effortlessly. Nobody will know where she is. The porter drops her bags on the floor of Compartment C on the *Algonquin Park*, the very end car of the train. She hands the porter a Canadian five-dollar bill; he holds it up by the tail and sneers at it and seems to be about to throw it off the train. Or maybe just drop it on the floor and step on its head and put it out of its misery. Finally he tucks it in his red jacket pocket and exits like a stage direction. Alone (at last). The pause of waiting and halted, frozen departure. Not quite going yet, but with one wheel almost going and the train paused, poised, just about to. Just about to. She looks at herself in the triple mirror over the dressing table. "I love this hat," she says to her trinity of personalities. "I just love this goddamn hat."

Enter the Hero; Long Shot

The dressing table has three mirrors, all of them accurate as gunsights. The train shrieks around the curves of the Fraser Canyon and she puts her shoes up where it says *Chaussures* and her bags up where it says, she thinks, *Les Bags*; and all that French is just another reassurance that she's in *another country*, a border between her and all those debts, and so it's safe now to go out to the lounge for a drink. The passengers back there are gasping as they look over the immense and serious drops of the Fraser Canyon, down into the recesses of China Bar — the sunlight sinking and gurgling as if it were leaking away down some celestial drainpipe — and she suddenly feels that the train is stopping. It must stop itself car by car in a long series of blue vertebral halts. A small sign stands up beside the track; it says CHINA BAR. She sees a man in a fedora and a big long dirty coat swing aboard the train two cars ahead, carrying a grip.

Why has the train stopped for this man?

For the plot, of course.

For the plot and for the polarity, for his battered case and his face and his way of occupying space; that's why the train stopped. Hiatus. Pause. Pause steam, pause wheels, pause *whistle!* And starts and repeated starts all down the cars. They are moving forward again, in a long series of blue vertebral charges into Hell's Gate. And suddenly she is assured that this Canadian train, with its end panels showing Acadian farmers with baskets of apples, cheeky blonde equestriennes riding behind a guide through the Rocky Mountains, all done in tones of grey and pink and Rose of Sharon sometime in the middle fifties, is invested with a *romantic presence*. Like the man in the Camel advertisements; like photographs of photographers taking photographs surrounded by admiring Pathans; like lies, prevarications, inventions, illusions, stories, pacifiers, anything you can think of that causes human beings to act like idiots; a *romantic presence*.

Remember That; See Your Diagram

See your diagram for the mystery to unfold satisfactorily.

On page three is a diagram of the last car on the transcontinental, one of the old Park cars with their aging 1950s splendours. There is a sunken bar behind frosted glass, the glass depicting Canadian ducks being startled totally out of their wits by some unseen and ominous presence; and in the lounge area are armchairs made of pink carpeting and tube steel, newspapers and battered ashtrays. The end of the car is round, with a porch, the place from which movie stars and royalty used to wave or declaim things to each other. There are also, in the end car, four bedroom compartments: A, B, C and D. Hers is Compartment C. Remember that.

And when she saw him get on the train at China Bar, she quickly slammed shut her window blind and turned around, and surprised herself in the full-length mirror on the back of the door. She picked up her pillbox hat and put it on her head as if it would save her from poverty and tallness and old age, from death and lonesomeness, from all the terrors of Hell's Gate, which they are rapidly approaching.

(Well, *something* does. *Something's* got to save you. Why not a hat?)

Get the diagram and check it out, because it is here the drama will be played out, as in a game of Clue; the reader is supplied with a diagram that can be seen as the various compartments of the reader's mind, where huge symbols and stereotypes crash into each other, run in and out of the doors of the left and right brain, blundering like butlers and detectives, vamps and rich widows, a Western Union girl in saddle shoes and Mr. Boddy, without whom none of us would be here.

"Ladies and gentlemen, in a little while we'll be passing through Hell's Gate," says the conductor, ripping off half their computer tickets with wild abandon, and everybody loooooookkkkkksss out.

A Shit Job

He is reading a report when he hears the train approaching in the distance. It has to slow down at China Bar, that offbeat bottleneck in the Fraser Canyon, a heart in a slow artery. All around him his story exists like boxcars, with no effort. He has not constructed his own story; it was done for him, effortlessly; the image is comfortable so why struggle? The paper is crackling and trying to escape in the rising wind of the canyon. The report says:

This woman appears to be travelling across Canada by train, posing as a railroad detective, claiming to solve mysteries that not only have the other passengers not seen as mysteries at all, but in which they are completely uninterested, such as:

> *Who are we, really?*
> *Why are we here?*
> *Where are we going?*
> *What is the purpose of your life? and*
> *Why am I asking you this?*

This woman appears to be travelling

She is usually dressed in vintage hats, suits, as well as expensive and tasteless haute couture: evidence of fraud. She is not always dangerous if apprehended, not always alert if questioned, not always defensive if accused, and is not always broke or fired, but usually. Maybe continuing to use VISA, Mastercharge and American Express; will most likely disembark somewhere east of February carrying everything she owns in spite of herself.

What a shit job, he thinks. I can't really be doing this.

Instant Replay or: Can You Run That By Again?

And when she saw him swing onto the train at China Bar, she quickly slammed shut her window blind and turned around, and saw herself in the full-length mirror on the back of the door — NOW APPEARING — like a special attraction and a surprise. She picked up her pillbox hat and put it firmly on her head as if it would save her from tallness, from being old or dead or poor or lonesome, from all the suicidal terrors of Hell's Gate, which they are now approaching. (Well, *something*'s got to save you. Why not a hat?) And he seems to have seen her, his face shadowed by his hat brim, a five o'clock shadow, a six o'clock shape.

"Ladies and gentlemen, we are now passing through Hell's Gate," and everybody loooooooooookkksss out.

She steps out into the aisle and walks down to the bar behind the frosted glass, and says to the bartender:

"I'll have a rum and Karma-Kola."

The bars of sunlight are falling one after the other into the Fraser, falling like the slats of a venetian blind, and the Americans are already setting up the complex murder-mystery game called Clue. Someone will be found out, someone will be discovered in the hot ambushes of the *deed*, and one person or another will lose. There is some music playing, a series of notes like spring runoff, now freezing into fall, and the mountain poplars are spending their yellow coins like gamblers.

Delayed Images

The man who got on at China Bar walks into the club car; he walks down the aisle, puts his grip into Compartment D (remember that) and looks down to the bar beyond the frosted glass. And there she is:

> *Sitting in the Club Car Drinking Rum*
> *and Karma-Kola,*
> like a book title.
> Is this a detective novel or what?

His effortless story falls into place, a series of delayed images.
She continues to make hers up, spending her imaginative energy like a gambler.

A Railroad Dick

He sat down across from her and took off his hat, which was very old, and brushed off the front of his jacket, which was careworn, and looked at his watch, which was a big one with hands on it; and it was six-thirty in the evening. They were passing by the stone ramparts and foaming liquid theologies of Hell's Gate. She glanced out the window and thought about the mechanics of ending it all (all what? — it was something Lupe Velez never asked herself, caught between the sudden apostrophes of sunset and terror) and said to the man,

"But where are you really from?"

and he said,

"But why not from China Bar?"

and she said,

"Because it doesn't look like anybody really lives at China Bar, and because of your watch."

It was a shot in the dark, and she knew she was not likely to hit anything, not with the amount of dark she was shooting into.

"What about it?"

"It says seven-thirty. That means you've just dropped in from another time zone, say Alberta."

"Alberta," he said, agreeably. And then, "Right." And he asked her,

"Who are you?"

and she said,

"I'm a railroad dick."

Parentheses

(What, no opening gambits? Like:
  "Where are you going?"
  "Montreal. Where are *you* going?"
  "Same place. It's a long trip."
  "Three days and three nights. But it's nice having a compartment."
  "Yes, it is. I especially like having a compartment on this end car. They're the nicest ones."
  "Yes. There are only four of them." [See diagram.]
  Pause. Pause drink, pause squeal of wheels; hiatus.
  "Mine's C."
  "How odd. I'm in D."

They realize they are in for three days and three nights on the old Algonquin Park, over the mountains and the Connaught Tunnel, the Kicking Horse Pass, in for Calgary, Regina, Winnipeg, Thunder Bay, Toronto; in it for the duration, for what it's worth.

And of course they don't even ask what is behind in the way of a past or a marriage or a head of household; on trains you don't ask. Or if you do, expect anything. They expect everything. She will make up her own story in direct contradiction to what was made up for her; that is, to be little and grateful and hard-working, to please people, to escape a low-level job by marriage in which she would be hard-working and grateful and diminished into the littlest thoughts and actions that can be managed. He makes up his own story as an enhancement of the one that was made up for him; to be large and active, enterprising and heroic. So there you are. This is how they strike each other: like a match and a sandpaper surface. End of parentheses.)

A Classy Exit

"Oh, really?" He looks over at her hat and her tacky second-hand clothes and the mahogany mink: a jarring mix of signals. He takes her drink from the stand and sniffs it. "A railroad dick drinking some kind of cosmic Kool-Aid." They look out over the landscape, where the ground has risen up out of the Fraser Canyon toward more agreeable mountains. She takes stock; she is sitting in the club car beside a large, forty-ish man with a day's growth of beard and sweaty clothes who seems to be looking for something. Maybe he's lost his twin sister or his options; maybe he has a story that he's made up all by himself, but she doubts it. She wonders if he's going to turn out to be Dull Normal, and if he does, how she can get away. But he wants to know, "Have you ever arrested anybody?"

"Of course." She picks up her celestial cocktail, rising to the challenge of inventing another lie for yet another stranger. "I just arrested a guy last week for homicide in a no-homicide zone."

He snorts; it appears to be a form of laughter. "But aren't you supposed to find things out?"

She's got to think up something else here. Okay, she's got one; it's easy. "I just found out last week that Clark Gable had false teeth."

"Not bad," he says. "That's really not bad."

Oh bizarro, she thinks. *This is turning into plain icky regular prose fiction.*

What can you do but get up and walk away from it when things are turning plain icky and regular?

"Excuse me," she says, and gets up and walks out of the bar in time to some very offbeat rhythms: a classy exit.

Left Alone

He asks the bartender for a drink from the first bottle his eyes light upon behind the bar. The train is going through evening like a detective through somebody's drawers. It's not interesting any more. There's a final and total indecency in the pursuit of American capital as it slides across the permeable border, even when the pursuit is as arresting as this one. Pursuits have to be worth it; there's got to be something at the end that will make you bigger or more complicated than you were, something that is unambiguously rewarding. In his crude pursuits and captures there has always been the chance of looking at the performances of fright or regret, naked people thinking naked thoughts. At this point he doesn't believe he could detect elephant shit in a henhouse. He leaves everything leavable on the table (peanuts, change, a clue), a fort deserted in panic or boredom; he walks away from the Americans playing at butlers and fiends toward Compartment D. Remember that.

Kicking Horse

We've all had our moments of terror. They are usually when (a) we think we may be killed and (b) we think we may be taken for who we really are.

That night they move through Salmon Arm and Revelstoke; they are through Roger's Pass and are now climbing the grade toward Kicking Horse, the highest pass at the spine of the Rockies. They have gone into the spiral tunnel moving upwards, the laborious train moving and moving upwards, and she dreams of The Man from China Bar. She dreams he has a list of questions for her; she dreams he has a watch that always says an hour ahead of the real time, that inside his watch night is moving forward faster and faster, accelerating, infinitely accelerating, as if they were on the edge of a black hole, as if they were detectives researching the possibility of infinite night! She dreams his face is hidden under the brim of his hat; she dreams her own face is hidden behind her veil; she dreams the train is moving upwards and always upwards through the spiral tunnel toward Kicking Horse Pass, and then suddenly and horribly dreams that her ears are bleeding, that her pillow is covered in blood; and she says something very loud and sits upright, throwing the pink woollen Canadian Pacific blankets on the floor; and the train is turning on itself inside the spiral tunnel, introverted, clanking and jerking. The porter knocks on the door and says,

"Ma'am, are you alright?"

The Man from China Bar can't help but hear all this through the thin panelling; he hears her say,

"Oh yes? What's wrong?"

and he says,

"You must have had a nightmare, ma'am,"

and she says,

"Well, what was it about, do you think?"

and he says,

"Ma'am, I have no idea,"

and she says,

"But wait, where are we now?"

and the porter says,

"In a spiral tunnel in the heart of a mountain, moving upwards toward the day, toward a very high pass in the peaks, and we'll be there soon, and we'll stop briefly to take on a cargo of light, so be of good heart, my darling, and do not be afraid, because we will not be going around in circles in the dark forever," and she says, "Oh, I'm so glad." Rocked on the slow climbing of the coaches and all their hubcap-shaped wheels, eight to a car.

Over the Kicking Horse

Porters in their red jackets move smoothly and efficiently throughout the train — the Ministers of Sleep and Dreams, with their small packages of soap and matches, and their penlights, towels and toilet paper — silently handing out in the night all your images and nightmares. Men of great circumspection, stepping without noise on their crepe soles, carefully, with a sense of *movement*: of a train and of *moving persons*. When the train emerges from the spiral tunnel and at last reaches the top of Kicking Horse Pass, they walk to the aisle windows and look downwards in the glittering high-altitude moonlight to the three different levels of track below.

And then they go on, moving down the racketing and rolling train while outside the windows on either side there is an infinitude of spaces and peaks, with an edgy shine to it all, generative, like a mind in near space, cloud banks foaming in the moonlight below as if here — at the top of the Canadian Rockies — was where all the weather of North America were generated: this is where clouds are manufactured; this is where lightning is forged; this is where rain is distilled in long, flashing tubes of moon; the mint where snowstorms are printed and impressed, where sundogs are cobbled and walked off with like the shoes of the sun in reaching twenty-four hour steps. The porters move silently with flashlights from car to car, dispensing dreams and nightmares, picking up the tossed blankets of the sleeping-car passengers and regretting the tortuous positions in coach, whispering, "Be of good heart, my darlings, there are miles of it, and it is still the same Earth."

'Ti' Déjeuner

The first call for breakfast serves as a wake-up call for those who have come from British Columbia: the shocking voice of the dining car attendant as he storms through the sleeping cars, "FIRST CALL FOR BREAKFAST, PREMIER APPEL POUR LE 'TI' DÉJEUNER!!" urgent and controlled, as if you must wake up now! Or forever miss the town of Canmore with its bare November trees full of wrens; the arena; a gabled house with a red Toyota in front; a cowboy on a bicycle.

(They passed a freight in the early dawn light, and the rhythm of sunflashes between the cars was a pulse; it awakened him briefly, leaving him with the impression of discontinuity and the sensuous arrival of day. What's his story? Where's he really from? For that matter, where are *you* really from? What are these long argyle socks doing in the sink, drooping over the edge, plaid pythons; and what are the rattling crashes of the window frames doing waking him so early, the drumming passage of a freight, or was it the dining-car attendant with the piercing voice whom he would like, right now, to strangle? He turns over in bed, he hears her turning over in bed; he imagines they are facing each other through the thin panelling as if they were in two different frames of a love comic.)

Addresses: The Man From China Bar

His address is, at this point, nothing but train. On a stretch of bad track his entire past falls out of the overhead rack and spills on the floor like underwear or playing cards.

"Drop something in there, sir?" says the porter, who was passing by out in the aisle.

"Yes but it's alright," says The Man from China Bar. Lying on the carpet is his identification, the real one, and his purposes, which are large and high-calibre. He shoves it all back into his suitcase. He looks at his shoelaces, which cross each other like two single-minded arguments, and wonders how he got here, wearing feet like this.

Our Heroine at a Disadvantage

On the morning of the first day after the first night on the train, she comes up out of vital nightmares about large, empty containers. She has such a hard time with herself: the self that was delighted as a Christmas child with the cornucopia of plastic cash; the self that was hidden behind a hat (O Karma! O Maya! O Illusion! O This! O That! O the Other!); and the self that can be toted up on a running balance at the bank, the credit companies, all those organizations that have your number; and the self that goes riding on trains, the one that sat in the club car the night before drinking rum and Karma-Kola; and another, startling self that opens your compartment door and then closes the door behind it, saying,

"Good morning," and hands her a styrofoam cup of coffee. And the self that says,

"What are you doing in my compartment?"
And the self that says,

"You should keep your door locked. I came to see if you were going to breakfast. And I see you aren't yet, or you'd be dressed."

If somebody does something unacceptable and yet hands you a gift, like a cup of coffee, at the same time, you are very likely to take the gift and your anger will defuse, go out, be rained on by the generosity of his hand with the coffee in it. He settles himself comfortably on the floor in the corner, apologetic and sincere, in a rattling patch of sunshine. She tries to drink the coffee without letting the sheet slide down, and the train is following its natural bent toward Calgary. What the hell is she supposed to do? Talk? Be intelligent?

"Well, I am going to breakfast but why don't you leave first, and then I can get dressed."

"Drink your coffee," he says, "and give me the cup."

She's at a disadvantage; she can't remember people very often seeking her out and giving her something, although she has worked very hard at giving the opposite impression. They have both worked very hard at making themselves into the right stereotype. Neither one of them has always been completely successful.

Lying on Trains

They are still up in the mountains; the engineer has decided to gain the time they lost coming over Kicking Horse and is pressing the red zone. They are rocketing along the Bow River at an awesome rate of speed, and The Man from China Bar opens the hard-to-open 1953 door for her into the snow-powdered vestibule, where everything is candied with frost and glaze, and the next car is a Pullman; they pass the bunks and bunks of sleepy people, and the beautiful old fading colours of Canadian trains, and the sleeper's *ultramonde* hues and tints of dreams that are just now sliding away into breakfast.

"But what do you do for a living?" she asks The Man from China Bar. They stand at the entrance to the dining car, hesitant as fish entering new rapids.

"Sound," he says. "I was a sound techie on an Australian movie last winter."

"I don't believe it," she says. "People always lie so terribly on trains."

And she heard him laughing.

Instant Replay

S he doesn't have on all that vintage 1940s today. All she
wanted was that scene, that one scene that had been grow-
ing in her mind for months; she calls it *boarding the train*. Now
she's wearing expensive labels and other clothes she bought
on charge accounts after she got fired, after she left him, after
she decided. This is when clothiers make a lot of money off
women like her, and why not? There's nothing wrong with
Royal Robbins that a little money wouldn't cure. Her hair falls
down her back like a lot of wilderness resisting agriculture.

"Sound," he says as the waiter ushers them to a table. "I was
head sound techie on the Australian film a year ago this fall."

"I don't believe it," she says. "People always lie so subtly on
trains."

And she could hear him laughing.

Breakfast in Canada

As they are having their revolting breakfast (because if there's one thing Canadian trains haven't yet figured out, it's the existence of good food) they watch the other sleepy people around them: people from the sleeping cars smoothing their hair, the ones from coach looking as if they had spent the night in a duck press. She and he gaze out of the armour of their stereotypes as the Bow River slides past in as many loops as a snake might exhibit locked in its winter tangle, in all the colours between green and indigo, cascading toward the low, glossy, yellow-and-white prairie landscape — *so Canadian*, so utterly cherishable, like pear cider, like a photograph of your mother when she was twenty-one — and she is telling him all about herself.

"When I was little, in Missouri, my cousin Rita Jean and me used to be put to bed together out on my Aunt Hetty's back porch, and we would talk about getting out of Missouri, and where we would go, and what we would do if we got out. The trouble was, we didn't know what we would *do*."

"A lot of people have that trouble and don't even know it."

"Yes, exactly, that's what I told Rita Jean. And we didn't know what kind of men we were supposed to try to get and marry us, outside of the kind of men we were raised with, and if they didn't beat you up and they let you drive the car, what else could you want?"

"Nothing, obviously."

"And we used to lay there in my Aunt Hetty's feather bed out on the back porch, sleeping out there even in the middle of winter, and the feather bed was so deep we'd have to holler at each other across the puffs of it; it was like talking to each other on the telephone. And we could see all the winter stars, and we could see the pear tree by the pond with the little pear twigs all sticking around like fish bones and the stars blossoming in them instead of pear flowers, and we'd say, 'If I ever get out of Cooper County I ain't never coming back.'"

"Well, did you?"

"Oh, I go back all the time!"

It occurs to her they are speeding through counties right now, all of which people want to leave, or some do; or do they have counties in Canada?

"Do you all have counties in Canada?"

"Sometimes."

He listens so carefully, watching her drink coffee, that she thinks he may be comparing her to a description in some report that says she skipped out on $50,000 worth of bad paper. Suddenly she feels she should explain everything about her life, so he would understand why she skipped out on $50,000 worth of bad paper, but she doesn't. *Stop imagining things*, she tells herself. *On the other hand, if I stopped imagining things, I never would have done this; life would be dreadful. But anyway, he's just an attractive man that happened to get on the* 40 · *same train I did, is all.*

"What else do you do besides sound?" she asks.

"That's all. Sound. I listen my way through life."

A Heart in Reserve

The dining car moves with the heated steams of cooks and heavy railroad silver — old Canadian Pacific silver — and you can get breakfast splits of champagne if you really push it, because behind all the frosted glass etched with kingfishers and meadowlarks and the man in Canadian Pacific's old Tuscan-red jacket, there's that apparent and careful sobriety of a northern country. Only the Trans-Siberian runs a longer distance, and at what cost! But after sobriety comes a deeper sobriety, that of a final, happy gaiety that comes when you know you've stepped off some edge, a tectonic plate; you're running headlong across a continent and being served breakfast at the same time. She's an African Queen, and if she's careful, she keeps a heart in reserve.

"I thought you would be interesting when I saw you," he said, "and you are."

How can she resist this?

What does he mean, *interesting*?

Inventing Your Own Story

The Man from China Bar says he has spent the summer, after doing the sound for the Australian movie, trying to shoot the Fraser in a Volvo. That's why he was at China Bar. Now, for the first time, he finds himself having to invent his own story; in opposition to the one that was made up for him. Make it up, single-handed—without the cooperation of secretaries, mothers, wives, girlfriends, advertising—and suddenly he wants to tell her, *I didn't used to be this way. I had a different job at one time and then something happened. I didn't always have this occupation.*

He glances at her; maybe it's not her. Maybe the woman he's looking for is really evil, a chippy as it were, a professional who knows how to juggle credit cards and forge signatures, a nasty Seattle booster, a paperhanger, somebody with a dull creepy mind who labels everyone she knows as either *a scumbag* or *a real sweetheart*; someone he could simply arrest in midflight and return to the authorities and the credit companies. *I didn't always have this occupation,* he wants to tell her. He wants to invent a story as to why he took it up. A tragedy in his past somewhere. Like Dashiell Hammett had tragedies. Or invented them. He watches her suddenly grow nervous and light another cigarette, look at him and then look away.

"Where are we now?" she asks, looking out.

"We just passed through a town called Harris." He pushes the plate of sliced fruit toward her. "Eat your breakfast. This may be the last mango in Harris."

She bursts out laughing, spewing smoke, and he thinks: *It can't be her.*

Railroad Silver

S he wants to get out of breakfast. The Man from China Bar sits there with his past around him — uncertain and suspended, as hers is — like those of everybody on the train. If one were to note down what was really said it would read like a musical score, rushing toward Calgary. But he says very little. This is because he's a soundman, probably. And in his silences she will talk too much. Or say something factual even when she doesn't mean it. She gets up from the steam and the carnations, the heavy cups and the thin waiters and the railroad silver, the glossy flat landscape and the coiling loops of the Bow River — which has apparently fallen out of heaven just as it is, a celestial lariat, suddenly frightened — and says,

"Really, I must get back to my compartment and write some letters."

And he says,

"Something's wrong. I can hear it in your voice."

And in his head he says, *Wherever you're from, don't be from Seattle.*

And she says,

"Yes, well, sometime you must describe it to me. I can't really hear the sound of my own voice."

On Hold

S he feels they've been sitting in the Calgary train station too long. She's getting nervous; she is wondering if somebody has spotted her and they're waiting for confirmation of her description from the credit companies or something? Are we moving yet? Is anything going to happen yet? Her life is turning into a hood ornament. She looks out at Calgary, what she can see of it. The Husky Tower points upwards over the train station and then saddles itself with a concrete toilet seat. Downtown Calgary appears to have been built over Labour Day weekend out of shiny stuff. The train is still halted; has been for hours. They are suspended; prepared to go but not moving. It is as if it were midnight of the New Year when something is supposed to change forever, if only the whole train of the year's months would move forward. By the time they get to where they're going all the passengers will be jaded with movement and noises, but now everybody is thinking, *Let's go*. There is one last passenger running down the concrete apron, and steam whistling from between the wheel's teeth; far forward some men in blue uniforms are loading frozen cardboard boxes onto the dining car. The moment of leaving seems to stretch itself like a celestial synthetic. Who was that man?

Royal Flush

The signs say *Ne flushez pas le toilette quand le tren est standing en gare if you don't want to get in real trouble, comprenez?* or something like that — her French is high school — but she *always* forgets and she's flushed it anyhow. What can she say? Shout "Sorry!!" out the window? Eventually they pull out of the Calgary station just past lunchtime.

Were these the secrets that Claudette Colbert and Clark Gable knew? And never told us about? The oddities of travelling by train across a bilingual continent. It happened one night. Outside her window sixty pronghorn antelope go springing across a yellow-and-white world, printing and printing with their tiny hooves the perpetual message of endangered species, like hearts, the words: *Honey, you're going to miss me when I'm gone.*

Letter

She writes a letter, not to be mailed, but to create a second person singular, a "You." She is inventing somebody to take the place of an absence, to whom she can leave all the agency, where she can place all the blame. She doesn't know that "You" is the most dangerous address in the universe. Just listen:

"I used to wake up from these horrible dreams and you would be there, I used to struggle to bring us both out of our separate sleeps so that you could comfort me, I used to swim and swim toward the surface — it was always up there some- where — I wanted so badly to be rescued and you were always rescuing everybody but me.

"I'll meet you there in Montreal and we will go to *Les Filles du Roi* and have the most unbelievable food, and we will look at each other across the table, through all that candlelight and its colours of banana and gilt — I will still be rocking a little bit from the train — and then we will get into an argument about who's paying for the dinner! *You're* paying for it, and for another dinner if I want it, and another one after that, and if you ask what my life has meant to me so far, I'll tell you that not only do I want to be loved, but I want to be rich. So drop dead."

Oh what a character I have invented, she thinks, putting down her Parker. The pillbox hat with the little veil is lying on the chair. She's looking out at the last of the Bow River and all those earth-and-redwood coloured condos just outside Calgary that look like desert camouflage bunkers, and thinks: *Nobody can get me on the phone or otherwise.*

Transition

The train is a universe that moves and jangles through a perfectly still landscape, creating apparent storms, a tunnel of shakes, a dimension of crackerjack efficiencies. The cook sharpens his long knives in the kitchen dining car with steely crashing noises, and the meat he is about to slice lies quivering on the counter: helpless and appalled. You can look up from your dinner and see the Cypress Hills, bald and blue, like friendly and curious asteroids peeking up just above the horizon that might at any moment turn feral and start to attack. Because of this she suggests they go back to the lounge car and read magazines.

Getting Yourself Together

She knows it's very important *exactly* how the lips are shaped, width of hips, positioning and colour of eyes. She sits in front of the triple mirrors over the dressing table and checks it out; she's always checking it out. It is as if she were personally responsible before the presumed male observer for every jointure and colour, as if she has put herself together single-handedly, as if she has bought herself at a big downtown Seattle store, charged herself on a credit card — probably at the cosmetics counter, Estée Lauder — watching with satisfaction and a sense of fury and courage as the metal imprinter, like a miniature rolling mill creating her presence out of cosmetics, mink, and plastic cash, racketed across the gold-and-blue card: *crash crash* and there you are! A nose, eyes, you got it, the whole manufactured face, the body beautifully designed. Outside, Alberta is sliding off toward a province called *Saskatchewan*; she's not even sure how to pronounce it. Her adventurousness has outrun her fund of general knowledge. The train jumps sideways and her eyeliner runs a long streak up her temple. *Watch it!* She was thinking about The Man from China Bar. *I want somebody to look into my eyes and want me. I want somebody to choose me and nobody else but me out of a crowd of people, out of all these passengers on this train, a man to walk into my life big as destiny and purpose, out of all these people on this train.*

Scarlett, Rhett, and a cast of thousands.

Am I beautiful? Almost beautiful? Not beautiful enough?

Flashback: The Background

S he surrounded herself with the right images: travel calendars, framed posters, can't get enough of those contemporary novels (*The Pill Dolls* and *Dying for Some*); she read *Esquire* to catch up on what the New Man is thinking about: money, sometimes. Women. *I want to stay at the Lancaster in Paris, which epitomizes the discreet wealth and good manners of its setting on the Right Bank, but I don't want to stay at a replica of the Lancaster in brash Houston or Dallas, as that Texas millionairess would have me do. An instructive example, again, is Haiti. Despite its position on a hill at the end of a drive, the ramshackle Oloffson embraces the colorful squalor outside its gates.* Hotels. The New Man is thinking about hotels and colourful squalor. If you get up in the morning and read this while you have your coffee and look at the pictures, it will make you shiny. She works in a low-grade job at a Seattle television news station; her friends are all pissed off at her — *"She's in such a terrible mood these days,"* they say, and ram pushpins through heads of state. Taking the bus home at night, wearing pink plastic Chinese shoes, she can see whole sections of Seattle laid out, and the lights in the median darkness and drifting rain show up her face in the bus window, her terrible energy shining out like the teeth of Lucifer. The lost temper: where do tempers go when you lose them? Her ideas don't have any whole connections; they fall out in sections and terraces like Japanese land usage. When they all go to the bar after work, she thinks, *Wanda's not talking to me, she's afraid I'll start in on that Japanese land-usage thing. But it was a good story idea, I know it was. But researchers aren't* supposed to have good story ideas, we're supposed to research. She is smart enough to feel it starting: the resentment and bitterness that will soon simply become normal. She should get on a train and go somewhere — the Orient Express, the Trans-Siberian — like Vanessa Redgrave or Vivien Leigh, maybe up in Canada across the Rockies. And then get into a fast skid of invention, all the people and colourful squalor she ever wanted to invent. Offices! Offices! Thousands of women in offices! With a grade twelve education she'll be here forever; the only way she could be more stuck is if she had two grade twelve educations. City College anybody? Life is really sixty-forty at this point; flipping furiously through the newspaper files looking for something. A head of state. She wants to know how to perform with grace under stress, like Butterfly McQueen or Mae West. If only she had less debt, more money, more grace, less stress. Shirley and Wanda review their personality amputations with pride. "I used to want to," says Shirley. "But now I realize that." Wanda confesses that she "used to think you could" and laughs over her coffee, "Ha ha isn't that just the way you think when you're a teenager? You think the world's your ... you know what." They have put so much effort into acquiring new and better personalities; she regards them with rage, crushing Lifesavers between her cute teeth.

50 ·

∿ AQUARIUS ∿

Travel is favoured if you keep a tight lid on expenditures, but don't let the cat out of the bag, especially concerning career interests. Romance and leisure activities will be fulfilling if you just don't let the cat out of the bag. YOU BORN TODAY remember you may not get born again so lucky; maybe next time in the middle of a war. At times bouts of temperament can throw you off balance, for you're somewhat high-strung and can sometimes be observed throwing the office potted plants out the fourth-storey window. Not really. Just kidding. Travel is favoured if you can buy all the tickets on credit cards. Birthday of: Paulette Goddard, Franchot Tone, Irwin Shaw.

Shirley and Wanda and Our Heroine go to the bar after work, and Our Heroine practises what she thinks of as her new bland personality: respond only, never initiate. It seems to please everybody, including one of the reporters she's been trying to get a date with. Seeing this, appalled by its success, she gets up and leaves, goes directly to a travel agency and buys as many train tickets as she can in the shortest amount of time on every credit card she possesses. She will keep going. She will purchase a set of matched luggage and a fur coat. *Go for it*, she tells herself. She's going to run up debts of Third World proportions and what can they do about it? She'll be in Canada on a train. She's going to feel what it's like to be rich and not care what people think of you. Ever. To be totally graceless under stress, to be outrageous, to talk about any idea she wants to, to walk out of the world in a trail of fire.

Tree Shadows

She hopes we are inhabited by a soul, fired with purpose as an engine is fired with coal in a boiler. Oh look at the old days, and how they used to jive, and at what speed, and under what steams! The mystery is jumping in and out of these dimensions; and flying behind us as we emerge comes railroad silver, and pink plastic Chinese slippers, a knight in shining armour, French dictionaries, breakfast buns, the Three Wise Men, hair straightener, Hawaiian shell necklaces, Filipino coins and books like these, books on old trains with old photographs giving the names and numbers of the steam engines. They seem, like dinosaurs, about to sink into a sepia earth. She flips the page; a running series of tree shadows flies past the dining-car windows like a girl running a stick down a picket fence.

"I just picked it up in Vancouver at the train station," he says. "Something to read."

"But you got on at China Bar."

"That's right, I did, but I ..." and in those three dots lie many hidden purposes!

He's a son-of-a-gun with adventures in every pocket.

Later

Our Heroine is playing a three-way game of canasta in the bar, absorbed; she has to be engaged in something, the way vamps and butlers are always somewhere else when the action happens. He excuses himself and walks up the aisle and without furtiveness into Compartment C. He begins to go quickly and efficiently through her luggage. The most important is the zipper case where she keeps her identification cards, and he goes through them one after the other, noting at least three different names, listening all the time for possible footsteps in the corridor, looking at the dates and destinations on her amazing collection of train tickets (Jesus Christ, she's the *Flying Dutchman*) as well as the name, looking at matchbook covers (names of restaurants and motels, all of them either Seattle or Vancouver), labels on clothing (here is a stapled-on Day-Glo tag — definitely Salvation Army), running the edges of a thick diary against his thumb and several sheets of self-reflections, which of course contain nothing more than imprecations against people named Shirley and Wanda — as if typewriter fonts would do him any good — opening her makeup bag, reading the labels on medicine bottles, the dates and names of doctors and pharmacies (all Seattle), then putting it all back. There's an antique change purse with a fifty-drachma note, and then he goes through the credit cards with a sinking heart, realizing with horror — the dread that Percival never knew — that the object of pursuit was indeed within reach. Seven credit cards, in three different names, and only one of them her real and hidden name, which he assumes is the same name on the army-green American passport, recently acquired, and no stamps on it yet. Which means she has no intention of returning to the United States from Canada, and his mind runs out on the strands of a web of possibilities. Europe, Mexico, Greece, but probably not China. Her paperback novels are all in English; they have pictures of rich and beautiful women on the front. Her appointment book (leather binding, recently acquired and unworn — like the mink coat, the shoes, the gold jewellery — she seems to have created herself out of credit cards) has no appointments. There are no tropical-weight clothes and no raincoats. Compartment C is a treasure house of hot items. He looks up at the unopenable window and considers chucking it all out and suggesting *Start all over*. They are passing a freight going the other way and the bars of sunshine, light pulses, flash between the coal cars and the grain cars. He gazes at it for a moment, hypnotized by the Doppler effect of the screaming whistle.

Yes, there really is a body on this car.

Reaching for Fire

They are nearly at Moosomin; the evening is blue and shaky. He watches her play canasta and wonders if he can hear his watch tick even in this train noise. *I could just quit the job; that's one option.* He would like to have a different history and become somebody else, but he feels things like magazine advertisements (large, commanding men looking down at lithe, expensive women) and women's deference and the way they give him body space pressing him into one simple persona. He was supposed to have been an investigator of fraud, and fraud has always intrigued him, fraud and those who employ fraud as a device to obtain food, clothing, shelter, adventure, and a background. Their apparent fronts, like stage sets, designed to tell a charming and simple *fable*. But she is beginning to unnerve him; he's dropping things — his package of cigarettes, his matches — sitting across from her. He watches the bartender drift by on salary. The train is pulling him forward like a zipper and he's opening up; some idea, unnerving and eastbound, is unbuttoning itself. He doesn't like the way he sees thoughts moving in her, hard as little glaciers, sliding away into the geology of calculation and poverty of which he has no experience. She has the innocent and spontaneous savagery of the starved, in I. Miller shoes, and he can't even guess the label on the suit. Is it possible he has always shared the world with people like this? Maybe she's not seeing herself through his eyes! Will he have to share the visual field? He wants to reach across the intervening space and seize her wrist like paleolithic man reaching for fire. *Come on and let's get out of the whole system.* If he could get rid of the advertising, avoid the deference of women and the bartender, he could make up his own story instead of being forced to act out this one. After all, she hasn't embezzled anything. She hasn't held up a bank, not yet anyway. This isn't *Guns at Cyrano's.* She's guarded behind her glossy contemporary stereotype; she's loving every minute of being encased in that expensive binding like a book somebody is giving a big sell. He wants her to come out of the character she's playing. *Will you come out of there*, he would say to her, *and give me a straight answer?* (There is no straight answer.) But the story of his pursuit is becoming so compelling that he can't remember his ending. (There is no ending.) He thinks, only briefly, about being poor, and female. What if waiters no longer spoke to him in respectful, quiet tones; what if women no longer gave him way on the street but crowded him instead; what if nobody made up his bed, typed his letters; what if people didn't look away but stared at or through him? He watches her as she shuffles the deck, dealing cards to the Americans from Houston and New Orleans. *I could take it*, he tells himself. *I'm so tough I can tear matchbooks in half.* He tears a matchbook in half; well, she's not so fucking poor any longer, is she? He imagines himself interrogating her, relentlessly. *What's it like?* and *How do you survive it?* She will tell him,

he knows, the absolute truth, starting with the small details.

First Class

They were right. She's surrounded by small signals of admiration and respect. She can feel it; it's soft, sensual as expensive fur. It's either the clothes or the way people look at the clothes. It's a turn-on. They approach you, you don't have to approach them and she has to remember that she doesn't have to do anything — angle for attention, speak hurriedly or convincingly — she doesn't have to be eager to please people. They are putting themselves out to please her. Yes. This is the great unknown unspoken secret of North America: ladies don't work, women do. She doesn't have to talk about her job because interesting ladies don't have jobs. They have *interests*. She's read enough contemporary novels to pass for class. Men give her appreciative glances, especially with the mink, and she imagines she looks like a studio portrait of Gene Tierney and maybe she does. The man who got on at China Bar, for instance. He's asking her about *herself*. Which is flattering and also makes her nervous. Imagine that clammy little reporter back at the television station, allowing her to sit beside him, interrupting her in mid-sentence without even saying "excuse me," expecting her to nod appreciatively at his interruption; what crapola. It's late and towns are going past them like displays. He takes her hand and looks at the diamond-and-sapphire ring, runs his thumb over the inside fire and draws it out into his hand, then seems to have put it in his waistcoat pocket.

She looks down at the ring. It is empty. Its deep iridescence glows fiercely in the dark of his waistcoat.

"That's an amazing ring."

"I found it between the seats of a Greyhound bus."

"Going where?"

"To meet somebody. My friend. Last week, in Spokane. The man I'm seeing."

"Shit." He leans back in his chair and laughs. "Shit."

Fairy Tales

It's so hard to stop herself from pleasing people that she ends up talking to him late at night on the club car, even though she knows she should not be talking to anybody late at night on the club car, so in order to both please and avoid giving information she lies, as usual.

"I'm from Montreal," she says. "Oh well, no I'm not. Not really. I'm not really from Montreal but I'm going to Montreal." And she knows her seams are crooked and there's a run up the side of her stocking and there's no way to hide it. And she says, "I'm just *going* to Montreal. I'm from Seattle. And in Seattle ... well, I've quit my job. I mean, my interests. I got fed up with all my interests. You didn't really shoot the Fraser Canyon in a Volvo, did you? What does that mean, shooting a river? I quit my work and I feel terrible about it. Well, no, really, I didn't quit work. I got fired.

"I got fired and it was horrible; I hate getting fired. I was a producer. This is the third time I've been fired in my entire life. And I've got family in St. Louis and I might go there if I want to. There's a restaurant there on the levee, it's a wonderful place, and I might go there from Montreal if I felt like it. If I had a train ticket I'd go there. But this is all really kind of stupid and lame, isn't it? It's kind of what you call a wet story.

"But that's what television is about. News, even; it's about making up stories. I could make up a story about this Karma-Kola, you know, about where it came from, some springs high up on a mountain in British Columbia, and a trapper who was dying of thirst and he found it and it was carbonated, and he couldn't drink it. And it was the real fountain of truth and he goes *ick, croak* and cacks out right there … Oh well, that's kind of gruesome, isn't it? I mean, it's just gruesome. And she s-t-a-n-d-s up and smashes out her cigarette as if she were following stage directions.

Escape Plans

She knew she would meet a man on the train. It's part of the script. Of course there are men on trains every day all over the continent. But.

She gets out the diagrams showing the layout of the Park cars, the dining car, the baggage and coach and the club car, far forward. How can we compartmentalize our lives, and everything? Are these things really blueprints that assure us nothing surprising will ever happen? Searching the diagrams carefully, we see that there are no people in them, only places for people. Coach seats and lounge chairs, little tables in the bar cars, the fold-out beds in the sleeping cars and the dressing tables, toilets, mirrors — there is something Pompeian about this, this empty ghostly train making its black-and-white way across Canada. A train made of diagrams, where spectres experience only the expected experiences, think the fashionable thoughts of their generation of spectres. There is seating only for people exactly like themselves who move like trains on predictable tracks, dwindling into the distance, lonely, and dead.

It is evening. Small beautiful things are happening overhead like stars. There isn't anything yet empty or wanting. She doesn't want him yet, and so nothing is spoiled. The Americans have fallen into novels and newspapers. She searches the diagrams, not for reassurance, but in case she would want to escape, hide, leap off the train.

A Reservation for Two

But here's the real horror story: she will have survived the nightmares and the ears, the murder in the club car, and the waiter, and arrived in Montreal; and she would have met him or somebody, and they will have gone to *Les Filles du Roi* and all its atmospherics in a taxi, and ordered dinner, only to find that she has been served *imitation crab* made out of pollock and fish cheeks! How can you ever know what you're getting? It's a question of money and its total lack of interest in the real thing; only prices. Maybe she'd better be happy she made it across Canada without being located by skip-tracers; that she has something to eat at all.

Cheating at Cards

He is almost angry that she would be like this, out of the rigid images of dry reports, or that his pursuit would become so reluctant, almost as if he were the one pursued. She could well rise in the night and get off at some prairie station, some tiny, remote galaxy of lights that would then disappear into the firmament of wheat. Maybe it wasn't her. And if it isn't her, of course, then it's somebody else. Why lie about it? They are playing ninety-nine, his fingers feel thick and inaccurate as he deals the deck between them.

"Tell me about doing the sound for that Australian movie," she says.

"It's complicated."

"Well, tell me the first thing you did when you went to work in the morning." She drops a one-eyed jack on him. "Jump-back jack."

"I walked up to Tina Turner, kissed her passionately, and then we had big danishes."

"What a job."

"There it is. Tell me the first thing you do when you go to work in the morning."

She remembers just in time she's a railroad detective.

"I walk into the Amtrak office and look around for the biggest man. I pick a guy and say, 'Come with me.' And we dress up in old clothes and go down to the rail yards and we start looking for hoboes. Sometimes we just ride around with the hoboes. We look for *clues*."

The Man held up all the face cards he had: a queen of spades, a king of diamonds, a jack of hearts. He held them up with their faces toward her.

"You know, sweetheart, someday you're going to have to tell all these nice people the truth."

Love Scene

Our Heroine is lying on the bed in her compartment, lonesome and subdued, wondering when it was she said the very last thing that went over the edge. The door opens. Enter THE MAN FROM CHINA BAR.

"I thought you might want some peanuts. They have wonderful peanuts on the train here in Canada."
"I had some peanuts."
"I thought you also might like this drink."
"I had too many already."
"It was an excuse to come into your compartment."
"Last time it was coffee. You're a regular catering service."
"Take the goddamn drink, will you?"
"I love masterful men."

Our Heroine takes the drink and sets is on the dressing table as if it were full of nitroglycerine. THE MAN FROM CHINA BAR moves stage left and sits on the bed.

"Have you noticed the enormous sexual energy generated on trains?"
"Yes, yes I have and it gives me goose pimples. Look at my arm."

THE MAN FROM CHINA BAR takes her arm and draws her down onto the bed. He tells himself to slow down. He slows down. She slows down. He feels like speeding up again and as a matter of *interest wonders if she travels around picking up men on trains. Not for the last two months, at least, he's sure of that, but anyway, in general. They kiss; it's Twentieth-Century Fox. The train jiggles and makes with the sound effects; lights flash by, it must be somewhere in Manitoba by now. Under all the exclusive labels she has a spare heart that works, and works, and works.*

Point of View

They begin to emerge out of the matrix of major stereotypes. They could have been symbols of anything: of male and female, of Canada and the United States, of refinement versus the untutored, of upper class and working class, child and adult, *sauvage* and urban. They could also be clichés of America's view of Canada as nothing but landscape. Of Canada's view of Americans as people who indulge in exotic squalor and high-rolling. They could be light and dark, love and hate, pursuit and flight, or approach and avoidance. They move into the hot sexual ambushes of the dark. The story is about somebody's body lying all along yours, somebody's mouth very close to your ear so that even the smallest whisper or intake of breath is heard clearly. Whisper of cloth, or no cloth.

Flowers on a Dark Background

She puts her arms around him and is afraid, briefly, that he will put his hands around her throat. And she is afraid he will wrap his hand around her arm above the elbow hard enough to bruise it. And she is afraid they might remember who they were before they took their clothes off.

Tarot: The Lovers

They are crossing borders in the night they did not even realize they had; moving into strange provinces, unconscious and alone beside one another in sleep, major and minor arcana, in their dreams, in their solitude — where in the territory of Earth are they now — if at all?

Silk Train

Trains move down wholesale on entire towns, running across complete landscapes, under the tall fantasies of farmers' clouds that refinish themselves each mile they move forward toward the other end of this place.

He finds himself plunging forward like a train, heavily, on a prescribed and circumscribed route, with intent; impressing himself on every landscape that arrives. It all has to be dealt with and catalogued, grasped quickly and then thrown behind him before something new arrives; something even more threatening. Little ties whipping by as if somebody were riffling the cards of a wooden deck, and for some reason neither one of them can let go without fear of being

Swept Away.

He has been imprinting himself on the world, making promises to arrive at stations at the right time; a man turns around only to find somebody has punched a hole in his ticket (It's a dirty job, etc.) and does this mean he's no good any-more? He hurries forward toward Montreal with a name and an address he could swear to in court, unlike her, as if Montreal were the Last Judgement and he were sure it was going to be in his favour.

Master Control

They woke up still barely west of Regina. They looked out and saw antelope fleeing like agile burglars, surprised in a cactus robbery. They are still sleepy, tangled in the thin old Canadian Pacific sheets, and the little light woollen blankets. They almost feel like captured bandits being transported across this existence to some vast, metropolitan dimension of another life, or what she would call *lifestyle*, heavy with stolen gold. As if they were captured but about to escape out of their stereotypes, stripping free, betraying their employers, their Master Control, rebelling, blowing their contracts.

He is not who she thinks he is. He has a history, an ex-wife, a grammar-school record, moments of which he is ashamed, memories of embarrassment and fear. They lie sleepy and groaning with early-morning aches; he has his habits, his knees, his socks, his obligations.

He sits up and pushes up the blind, his hand on her instep.

He says, "Where the hell are we?" and "Jesus Christ, are you smoking already?"

It's so hard to fall in love! It's harder not to fall in love. By this time they are coming towards Regina blowing a whistle, and the Americans have sat up with their game all night and apparently murdered somebody; not anybody you would want to know. (Probably another American; they are caught between violence and repentance; which do you want?)

Moving on the Margins

The Man from China Bar comes down the length of the sleeping cars carrying coffee, "excuse me, excuse me." He can't imagine why he got into this dalliance, especially with a suspect, except that it's wonderful. He can't imagine now why he ever took the job, running down the illegally rich, the border-line, the demented people who can't resist advertising, the ones who are addicted to the sound of the charge card's little printing press. "Excuse me." People who are moved by the gigantic images on movie screens, where everybody lives in an interesting tangle of problems; like his, and risk only their lives and not their money; like her. "Excuse me." Except people like this are just so much more interesting; he wants to find out what it's like when you're making up your own story, when you're not the centre of a precast myth, when nobody gives you deference and you do it single-handed. It's a dirty job but somebody's got to do it. Moving on the margins, a skip-tracer. "Excuse me, sorry."

Rules of the Game

The porter, full of stiff disapproval, has already made up the compartment and they sit, drinking coffee, watching the arrival of landscape. He takes out his pen and notebook and decides to make up his own rules.

Rules for Operatives in the Canadian Ajax Skip-Tracer Agency

1. Take local transportation when possible and charge it.
2. Remember everything you come across, and where it was put last, especially food, women, and bills of large denomination.
3. Write down vital signs in your notebook.
4. Drink whisky.
5. Get up front to the engine once in a while to see how Fate is running your life.
6. Never drink whisky on Wednesdays.
7. Dream dreams and write them down the next morning and interpret them the following night and stay away from other people's compartments, especially those of women suspects who glance at you over their magazines in the club car.
8. Dreams have reasons that are usually listed under number nine; they are thought out at the centre of the Earth, and then played out here, on the surface, in the red stone slot of the Fraser, in the North's blue snows, across sea-tone prairies; the armature of dreams and their strange vocabularies.
9. Fill in the blanks.

Repetition

Early morning; they approach the city of Winnipeg. "Many things have happened here," he says, "and a lot more might yet again and are now." She is ahistorical at this point, however, and doesn't care. The train is providing all the forward momentum in her life. After this? Europe, maybe, or Mexico. How would she get there? She'd go there and freelance news or something; maybe help all those hot-shit reporters from the television news teams. She's a good researcher. How do you think she figured out the credit-card scam? Researchers know strange things. She looks at him leaning back in the lounge armchair, a magazine on his lap, coffee; he's gazing out at the prairie and its lengthy silks running westward and yellow. His interesting large beaky nose and soiled tie, a scratchy morning shave and all the flat, two-dimensional images of sex and presence that people stand in front of them like enormous flexible paper dolls. She wonders if she's starting to get fed up: with being sober and being drunk, sick of being cool and tall and smart, tired of little pillbox hats with veils; she's tired of trains and yet she can't get off. It just keeps happening over and over; it just keeps happening over and over.

The Hudson's Bay Company

Winnipeg. They had an hour to walk down to Portage and Main where humanity, in a long procession, moves slowly out of the archives of the Hudson's Bay Company and disappears into postmodern slums. The factors, the Cree captains, the man who almost died on the long portage of the Sturgeon River, the man who wrote from the Hudson Bay Coast in 1679, "Snowing, blowing, shot a crow with one ball flying," a minimalist; and they watch as everybody God knew strolls past.

I could leave the train right now and dump this sleazoid, she thinks and wonders where would be the best place to hide; *maybe he's a skip-tracer.* She is getting more nervous. She could disappear into a department store, pose as a dress dummy as he runs around the cosmetics counters of Eaton's or Simpsons or the Bay; *she's slipped out of our grasp, lieutenant. Again.* Or she is caught; she would claim she'd never done anything like this before in her life. They'd let her off; *go straight, young woman.* But they happen to be strolling back toward the train station. It's Montreal or nothing. She'll get where she's going, not where she's forced to go.

Maybe they'll have caught up with her here. She's restless, waiting for the train to move, hiding in her compartment. At this point there is nothing anybody can do but go forward and prepare for what might come; the bald geography of prairies and the night. From now on she only has one road: it is like a New Year's resolution, simple and full of traps.

Detective Fiction

Well, it's a kind of minor form, a kind of minor plot — we slip in and out of phrases like waistcoats or clothes — a sly genre in which the subject of class is taken on and in which something has to be arranged for the pursuit and capture of a desired object.

Why do you have to have a plot at all; why not, as in legends, simply slide your characters forward on the smooth surface of gigantic contradictions, moving them forward as if on a train, placing each one carefully in correct clothes like paper dolls; the sex scenes are the ones in which the clothes fall off of them, if you remember playing with paper dolls. And how hard it was to keep the clothes on them, the pulp and paper romances you invented. You give them each a motivation, which will lead to the necessity of taking action; you construct the relationship, the background, the scenes of sex or intimacy or both (sunlight in rectangles falling through the compartment window on skin and lace and his cheap polyester tie in the sink, with flamingos on it), protagonists holding each other or their representatives (see my lawyer), her thighs open to him, his hand on her back, grasping each other's images, which will return like paper dolls to the printed page in the morning. The train is locked into a rigid schedule of train time, a series of halts and marches. And now Our Heroine and The Man from China Bar read magazines in the dome car; they talk in small, cautious sentences, commenting on the landscape. They could really give a big shit about the landscape. The bartender in his blue jacket regards them (another train romance) quietly above the elbow of his sunken bar behind the 1950s etched and frosted glass, arranging his Scotch, his wines, his rum both dark and light, and the high-pressure bottle of Karma-Kola. *Another train romance.* He watches them turn to each other, forming profiles. He passes by them with a tray of drinks and coffee (the American tour group is unfolding its characters again, all of whom are single-minded) and hears the low-tone laughter of Our Heroine and The Man from China Bar; a dialogue of whispers and jokes. It looks like they will be gliding into snow on the other side of Sudbury, tall bearded columns of descending frost. What really happens with train romances, detective novels, pursuit and flight? In these situations, does one really live only in the present instant? If so, we remain within the confines of the lyric, and if it goes on, then we have a plot, which makes a story. He said, she said, and who shot John. The bartender wonders who the story really belongs to — to himself, the marginal observer who is so dignified and deferential that nobody even notices his deference; to the porters, who make up beds; to the women on the train who support the work of loving and of conversations without even knowing they're doing it; or the white men who seem to be locked in privilege — or if a story is property at all and can be owned? The bartender is reticent and Jamaican, and so nobody has inquired enough to know that his mind is a sailboat made of magical disturbances, like all minds; and it is sailing sideways through the moving universe under a Genoa jib and full main. But the Americans want him to be The Butler again in their endless game of Clue, and again Mr. Boddy falters and dies, and again the vamps, the rich widows, the alcoholic uncles, the knives and lead pipes come into play as if they made a story merely by being there. The train moves eastward. The Man from China Bar listens to Our Heroine, who is talking about imaginary restaurants in Montreal; he is watching the faint, almost-snowing light on her hair and cheek, and her shoulders inside that swank silk blouse, for which, he knows, she has not yet paid.

Coming Out of It

The trees begin in eastern Manitoba in long fingers of forest, as if the jointure of prairie and the forest country had folded its hands together and were sitting in church, listening to a Protestant sermon on the sins of that madman Louis Riel. Through it all the train, with its architecture of speed, a housing of transient and expectant souls, crashes eastward. The stiff joints of the blue Canadian Pacific cars bend around the rare and remarkable curves. The train is throwing itself and its passengers recklessly into the rapid visual noise of the boreal rebellion, and the Lac Seul magic of Ojibwa revenge which is so sweet that passengers shooting through the town of Hudson fast as a World War II silk train think they have been blessed with a brief and strange perfume, like people being sprayed with testers at a cosmetics counter and only finding out later.

North Shore of Lake Superior: The Truth

The nature of absolute truth is that it is too boring to endure without a frontal lobotomy, and there is for most of us no virtue in it; and the universe is not putting out any daily editions anyhow that we can understand, and here's the Regina *Leader Post* among all the magazines and dailies in the lounge car — a blue little Prairie gazette, but what can you do? With its subtle Saskatchewan heart.

Truth is an absolute concept thought up after the invention of protracted and deliberate lying, which came shortly after the invention, not of speech, but of grammar. She reads the news-papers from Canada's major cities back in the lounge car. She considers taking up white-collar crime to take care of her debts, white-collar crime being the single lifetime adventure of accountants — double entries are their way of shooting rapids and smoking Camels — but she decides against it. She'd have to get a white-collar job first, and having an affair on a train isn't the way to go about that. Should she be an *adventuress*? She shakes out the Thunder Bay *Times-News* and discovers that a bush plane has disappeared in the subarctic somewhere to the north of them. *I bet you wish you'd taken a train,* she thought, but of course being an American she doesn't know that there are no trains up there. *Adventuress,* she thinks, remembering Paulette Goddard playing some exotic Metis character named Yvette with a knife in her teeth, who was rescued by a Mountie, the Mountie dressed in vast tentlike furs with tails of things hanging off all over him. *Adventuress, I love that word.* She looks out the lounge-car window; the train is racing south. *It goes with my hat.* The train thinks up more steam to say to the world like a smart-ass comment, speeding around the solid granite mountains of the North Shore, full of backchat and passengers. Oooooooooooooeeeeeeee, you can imagine it saying. Do your own soundtrack for this one. Do yourself a Doppler and imagine it, steam and all.

The Nature of Truth, Continued

Of course you can. Like a girl scout swearing on a tiny Bible, you just tell what you saw, an honest witness to the world's five-car pileup; you tell either what you saw or what happened to you, in sequence, in colour, in all honesty. Make yourself look good. Never mind the jury sitting here around the club car who have already been instructed by the bartender on the unreliability of eyewitnesses, even if you are being the eyewitness to your own life, or at least several aspects of your own life and all its dancing in ruby shoes (or what you think are ruby shoes). Or at least, you're doing the best you can. Or at least, well, bartender, bring me another rum and Karma-Kola. Tonight is my night. I'm going to go down to the *voiture-restaurant* and take my false self out to dinner and buy it anything it wants.

The train goes pelting through the darkness of the Great Lake shores, and her face shows up in the other side of the window glass. The dark side. It wasn't a lover as much as a job. She got fired from a Seattle television station and decided to go to Vancouver and take a train trip across the country: that's the plot. Something prosy and prewar. Someplace you could take liberties with reality, shore leave with the hard facts, running like a blind person over the Braille of Alberta's cryptic geography and the Canadian Shield and its several moons: the Oil Moon and the North Moon and the Blue Moons of Unemployment. The train charges down the tracks into the blackening happy night, down the typeface of the double rails and ties, as if it were a typewriter carriage engaged upon an endless sentence — all of it in uppercase, all of it in Helvetica Bold 48-point — typing out, like a transcontinental court reporter, **the truth, the whole truth, and nothing but the truth.**

Zen and the Art of Train Travel

The sound of one wheel remembering the times when it was in tandem with a lot of other interesting wheels, part of a herd of wheels, an unwashed mass of wheels, and how much they had to talk about, in a vocabulary of rusty howlings and hotboxes, a grammar of rotation and spheres, curves and straightaways, and how these two things meet and how sometimes they leave each other's company accompanied by terrible noises; like a congregation in the midst of a theological split.

Hubcap-shaped, massive, as if it had been poured solid into the mould, weighty as an anchor, the wheel is lying on its side devoid of movement, looking out with its axle eye at all the twisted, torn, ripped sheet metal sticking up into the air like the freeze-dried flags of a robot army: a derailed freight.

Nothing is safe. Anything that has forward momentum is at risk; and like all your years behind you the freights, with all that weight and tonnage, are strung out on lines of temporality. What is to stop it? Ever? The Man from China Bar thinks how, if anything were to bring him to a halt now, his entire life would pile up behind him and jackknife; he would catch fire; all those moments of passion being immense loads, like the year 1976. It would simply catapult right off the tracks. But he couldn't have lived without 1976, either.

Growing Up Rich in Oklahoma

They lie on their stomachs, smoking, watching out the frozen-over sill of the train window, watching the slow, lovely arrival of white lights in the distant towns presented by the horizon again and again, as if the lights had been turned on like theatres for their arrival; an appreciative audience.

"When we were in France," she says. "When I was eight."

"I thought you grew up poor in Missouri," he whispers suspiciously into her hair.

"Oh, that was a lie, I made that up. No, actually, I didn't. I have a friend who told me that. About her aunt and the feather ticks. And so I told it like it was me."

"So tell me a story about France."

"They have terrible cigarettes in France. The kind like we smoke are expensive."

"So you were smoking in France when you were eight years old."

"You've got to stop not believing me."

"I believe you! Right now I believe you."

They rush forward into all that naked geography. They hear the porter walking down the hall outside. It's one-thirty and almost everybody has gone to sleep except themselves; they are now in total possession of the train — they and the Americans, who are desperately trying to find out if it was Lauren Bacall, in the Caribbean.

She Thinks

I don't have to show anybody what love is; everybody should figure it out for themselves. Women are always going around showing men what "love" is, the way the moon shows Easter Week how to get out of April (straight through the almanac's corridor); we're supposed to guide and seduce them, open their fists into hands, and is it worth it? My own brain is in a fist half the time anyway; is it worth spending your whole life doing this? She thinks of him, without a guide, lost in the dense prose jungles of *She* and making squishing noises in the rainforest telephone booth where he is trying to dial MACHINE and BRUTE STRENGTH and WEAPON and CRUSH, or is he really? Maybe he thinks she would dial CLING and BLAME and MANIPULATE. Well, just let him! Look, look, he finally makes it out by dialling CIVILIZATION, with his heart in his left hand like a valentine, and herself on the train, rocketing toward Monday and November and Montreal. She lights up a cigarillo, blowing the tobacco fumes toward him, smoky as Chicago.

Lake Superior

The train has long windows that weep with frost, the train cries and cries and cries all the way around the north shore of Lake Superior. The train is a perpetual performance, a carnival, a traveling medicine show, a sort of genteel psych ward going around the bend. Far ahead you can see the engine, running very fast, following its own light like a soul being preceded through the gates of heaven or hell by the ferryman. We have come through Hell's Gate, haven't we? Well then. Down the aisles the porter steps on his crepe soles, with his flashlights shining, looking for strays; or for rents in the fabric of this moving universe, through which other porters inquire, with flashlights even more luminous than his. Occasionally he finds them.

The Third Night

They sit in his compartment, evening of the third night; they pass through the nameless villages of the Shield Country and the spruce standing endlessly to attention: the trinity of Church and Train Station and the Hudson's Bay with their lonely hard-rock night lights; and as in a stage set, everything is brief, perfect and understandable in one quick glance. In one town a group of people stand knee-deep in the harsh pool of station lights, grouped around a police car for some unknown reason, staring at the passing train with a disembodied expectancy that makes The Man from China Bar and Our Heroine almost feel *seen* or *waited for* by an audience or a reader waiting for their plots to unfold, not hidden in the rushes of their sexual attraction anymore; and the people at the station, like restless observers, saying *do something*. Then they have flown past — one of the women standing by the police car was holding a white duck. That's what she was doing.

Opening the Door to Strangers

She thinks about some kind of question to ask him; about himself. Men are such suckers for questions about themselves; and if you talk about your own thoughts they always interrupt you and so, like, don't fight it. To avoid having anything serious to do with this situation, she thinks about some kind of interested comment to make on his naked rib cage and she runs her fingers down his shoulder and arm. And if she has to say something about herself it will be something that makes her appear *absolutely normal and bland*. It will be a lie.

It will be something she either imagined or read in a book. She can't believe he's actually asking her questions about herself. He's too interested in her. But, of course, this is why detective fiction is as it is. In it, impossible things happen, like this one. She wonders why the hell she invited him into Compartment C. But haven't we all, at some time in our lives, voluntarily opened our compartments to strange visitors, wanting and yet not wanting, tempted and afraid? How the hell would she know? The train is really moving now, toward Sudbury and its acid rock. He wants to know about her shares in the Seattle television station and there's nothing to do but invent something.   · 89

Which Body?

And so she says, "Did you *ever* smoke?"

Because she's depending on the fact that men like to talk about themselves, and can always be deflected from unpleasant reality by same, and that he will tell her how he used to smoke, and how he quit, and how hard it was, and the way he figured out not to smoke, and he will give her advice on how not to smoke herself. This is only their second night together; maybe the last.

Her ashes fall on the Canadian Pacific sheets and she blows them away, like her feelings. And the pleasant, repetitive rhythm of passenger trains occurs and occurs, the feeling of violent forward movement. Moving into the future, the past strung out far behind across the continent like train smoke; but whose past was it, anyway?

"No, I never did."

She's got to look around for something else. "Are the Americans back there still playing Clue?"

"Yeah. And guess who joined them? An exotic dancer. She says she's going to Montreal and she's travelling with her pet snake. It's up in the baggage car."

"Oh gak!! You mean I'm traveling with a Canadian snake all the way to Montreal?"

"Which is worse: the snake or an imaginary body?"

"Depends," she says. She reaches over and strokes his stomach with all its hair. "Which body."

Explorers

He starts to try to explain everything to her.

"Look, there are such things as alternative universes. The one right next to us is extremely dull. It's called Blandworld. The people in it are worried if they're good enough for whatever, and the thing that keeps their universe going is that they never are. The world runs on the electricity of anxiety. I was a long, bulky yacht in my father's marina, and one day the anxiety wore through my lines and I just broke loose. I've been drifting ever since."

"That's very interesting," she says. "Isn't this just too, too utterly male and female? I tell you about my adolescence and you tell me about theories."

"I know." He sits the fedora on the back of his head. The train leaps from rail to rail, tearing sideways through Ontario. "I always had people looking after me. You can grow up thinking you're the centre of the universe but I'm not that stupid. People always deferring to you; it skews your brain. So I took a job. Actually, I have a shit job."

"Being a sound techie on major films doesn't sound so bad to me."

"Yeah, right." He has almost forgotten his story.

"Me too, you know. It's boring to come from a wealthy family. You get spoiled."

He throws some peanuts in his mouth, looks at his crummy shoes.

"People in Blandworld like to think they can keep everything calm, and that money insulates them against chance or fate, if only they could get enough of it. But by God, we're moving across some strange continents, aren't we?" He turns to her and smiles and what could she do but smile back?

Holograms on Parade

S he knows he is, in some way, moving in on her, so she becomes even more evasive by kissing him. She offers a false image. Maybe he'll be content with it; maybe he'll think it's the real thing. Meanwhile, like an animal discarding a leg in a trap, she'll become the mink she's wearing and disappear into the snow. She'll gather up her tracks behind her like glittering frozen bread crumbs. The false image turns whitely and runs its finger down his cheek, looking into his eyes, smiling. It bends forward and kisses him. "What's the matter," he says, holding her back. She is beginning to waver in and out of vision, like print when your eyes are tired. He's trying to remember when he learned that this sort of invitation, this sweetness, was an evasion. And he wants it at the same time. "I'm having a great time," he says. "Wish you were here." That's right. It was a postcard from the last person he didn't quite catch up with. A postcard with a raving beauty on the front. The postcard was from Peru. It said, *Bang*. A hot shot.

She Changes the Rules

While he is gone for coffee she goes swiftly and efficiently through his luggage, looking for who he *really* is. And if he's the wrong person she'll just rewrite his entire history for him. She finds a shaving kit with shaving stuff in it, all grotty with hairs, and matchbooks from all over the place. Maybe the train made him up, maybe the train supplied him with match-books from all the major cities of Canada. To be invented by a train! And his papers with an expense account (he was claiming all that rum and Karma-Kola; what a cheapskate! No flies on this boy) and a brochure for kayaks and canoes and canoe paddles. Also a clothing catalogue called *Cockpit*, which advertised a lot of World War II flying jackets — good God, here's the Vintage "Raider" Jacket: "Clark Gable wore one in the 1939 epic *Test Pilot*, flying Spencer Tracy's race-equipped P-35, and Harrison Ford wore a twin in *Raiders* ... special vintage effect of aged, timeworn leather in a completely new, handcrafted jacket." There you are; the guy's a loony. Or, maybe, a fellow loony. Searching through somebody's possessions in Compartment D is a low-grade occupation and she's properly ashamed of herself, but a full-time criminal can't be too careful. All his clothing labels are from one tailor in Victoria; that's taste. At least he hasn't got a Raider jacket. Although he must have been tempted. She checked the catalogue again. Actually the price wasn't bad. Never mind. Here, blood-freezingly enough, were rules for operatives in the Canadian Ajax Skip-Tracer Agency! Here you go; this is it. She reads the rules; he seems to have crossed them out and rewritten them. That was a good idea; she decides to add a few of her own:

9. Fill in the blanks as quickly as you can in the allotted time span; say seventy years.
10. Don't create beautiful suspects to chase on trains across Canada because they always evaporate at the end.
11. If this line of work doesn't suit you there's always unemployment insurance and retooling at the Ex-Skip-Tracer Rehabilitation Center in Spokane; they're doing great work with these people.
12. If you continue in this line of work you will be struck down by dread diseases and a special voodoo doll has been prepared for you and all who dare to follow the trail of MADAME ZONGA!

There. That ought to get the message across. The rules are always changing for whoever can rewrite them; following them is another matter.

Sticky Wickets

"Why in hell would anybody want to know that?" she says. This is getting ridiculous. Men can always be distracted from asking personal questions by asking them questions about themselves. She can do it like she can breathe. It gives her a sense of triumph and superiority. "You must have had a fascinating adolescence."

"No," he says. "I asked you."

Men never really want to talk about you unless you've broken the law or have appeared from outer space and are therefore an interesting scientific specimen.

"Where did you come up with seven different credit cards in three different names and which one is the real name?"

"What the hell, is it your business? No, I don't want to go to breakfast. And no, I'm not getting off at the next station. My girlfriends lent me their cards. Because I'm going to Montreal to do some shopping. I'm going to buy myself a Mountie. I hear they have them on discount. And I really don't want you in my compartment this morning."

She hears him through the thin panelling as though they were in two different frames of a Spiderman comic. She'll go to breakfast; that's where she said she wasn't going, so that's where she'll go.

Close Encounters

But she doesn't have enough cash for breakfast and she doesn't want to use the charge card again in the dining room. She'll think about all this in a little while; on a full stomach. Standing at the snack bar, looking tacky in high heels and the mink jacket, runs in her nylons, balancing a cup of coffee and a hot dog, potato chips — she finds she's afraid to try the VISA card even here. It's got to be him. He's a skip-tracer, a Mountie, a fed, a VISA or American Express detective of some kind, and he's going to say, *Okay, this is it; you're in it for fifty thousand dollars* and what can she say? *Just kidding?* It's the story of her life. Wage slave, going zombie at the television station research files again, in for life plus a year. Just kidding. She spills the coffee all over the mink and suddenly begins crying. *I want to be helpless and taken care of. I want to be just as depressed and lonesome as I want to be. I don't want to be a New Woman, not right now. I'll be a New Woman tomorrow. I don't want to be smart or strong or brave. Not right now. Oh well, forget it, everybody wants to go infantile from time to time.*

"But you can't do that, ma'am," said the man at the snack bar, tapping her wrist. "We don't take VISA at the snack bar."

"Oh yes!" she says. "Yes, sorry," and she gives him back the hot dog.

The man at the snack bar stands there with the hot dog in his hand, angry, watching the lady in mahogany mink make a fast exit into the vestibule. He turns and hands it to a ten-year-old from Biscotasing.

What He Doesn't Know

She remembers: "Where'd you get the ring?"

But if she acts like she doesn't know he knows, then he will all go away. It's hiding by putting your hands over your eyes; and then they laugh, and while they're laughing, you escape.

Life has required of her that she be on deck at all times, always on the periphery of her own story, with a full magazine. Your feelings never really count, not under those circumstances. Her exterior is expensive and shiny; it has cost her a lot of investment, time, and effort. It has done yeoman's service for years for both her and her employers. It is sturdy and canny; he doesn't know that, of course, and why should he?

"I didn't get it in the dining car, darling."

The Real Story

They are moving through the urban corridor of warehousing and industrial parks; she is being cool and straight. They are sitting in the dome car drinking rum and Karma-Kola and suddenly, as if struck by an inspiration, he says,

"You're not really a railroad dick,"

and she says,

"Of course not,"

and he says,

"You're not really going to meet anybody in Montreal, are you,"

and she says,

"No,"

and he says,

"You grew up just where you said you did, in Oklahoma," and she doesn't remember if she told him Oklahoma or not but she says,

"Yes,"

and he says,

"You're changing trains in Toronto and going on down to the Southern states on Amtrak,"

and she says,

"That's right,"

and he turns to her, taking hold of her wrist with a startling ferocity, and jerks her arm so hard the drink flies out of her hand, and he pulls her very close and says in his best low *Cockpit* voice,

"Listen you stupid little bitch, you're in it for fifty thousand dollars and everything seems just fine right now, but the problem is grand larceny, and if it's not me it'll be somebody else. You can't do this. You think it's a lark. You think all this is very high-rolling and exotic but in about thirty minutes you're going to wish like hell you'd kept on researching in that fucking Seattle television station or whatever it was you did there," and he gives her arm another jerk to get her attention because it appears she's faded off somewhere, into a world of bananas and guilt, and he says,

"You're going to take off to St. Louis and end up in some sleaze bar on the Landing eating imitation crab, thinking about who you'll call. You'll go through your address book and see who you know and you'll call them up and say, 'Come on down to Memphis with me. I got credit cards.' And you'll pick up some other sucker like me on the train, right?"
and she says,

"You know something, I've held down a job since I was seventeen years old and I got nothing to show for it but a train ticket to Memphis,"
and he says,

"And the other thing is, you're too old for anybody to teach you how to dress now,"
and she says,

"Come with me,"
and he says,

"I want to hit you. And you have crap spilled all over your blouse."

Cutting Off Her Credit

The suburbs of Toronto are going by, black and white, garrotted by snow.

"I'm sorry," he says, "that you aren't really a railroad dick. You would have made a wonderful railroad dick."

"Oh, but I am one," she says. "I travel on trains, don't I? I ask questions, don't I?"

"Come on," he says. "I want to show you something."

He takes her by the arm and they go down into the lounge car and out onto the vestibule. He takes her purse, opens it over her violent objections, removes the leather folder of credit cards, and starts pulling them out and whizzing them into the suburbs of Toronto. They fly sideways like little financial cleavers.

They stand looking at each other and every mile they move toward either taking each other into custody or parting forever.

Going For It

"Who the hell do you think you are?" she says, and doesn't wait for an answer. "Now I won't even be able to get a job!"

"Ah darling, do not fall further into the ranks of crime," he advises her. "It pays too well."

Every dream is an adventure story, detective fiction, a mass paperback with You as the protagonist but not quite; the trick is, which one of you? And in every detective story there is the point where you finally see the person pursuing you, and everything is clear to both of you, and you have to run.

Run from your fate, run down the aisle of the sleeping cars and the daynighter, through the vestibules, shoving at the massive and resistant doors, run through the forward club car, run for the baggage car, don't wear high heels, don't wear little hats with veils, don't carry sharp objects you could fall on, don't carry heavy baggage by the handle, don't fumble with old stories, don't wait for men who say *wait*! don't think about the past, don't get too involved. Don't be negative, just keep moving. The heroines of dreams and all their observations from moving cars.

The Action Scene

They're stalled in the Toronto train station, and he knows she's got to be breaking the sound barrier for the baggage car, and so he goes out the vestibule and down three steps like The Twentieth Century Limited. Hits the concrete and sees her, in that to-die dress and knock-'em-dead mink coat, jump up on the baggage cart like a gazelle. The baggage man asks her what the hell she thinks she's doing and, from all the available evidence, she tells him in no uncertain terms. She has a pigskin bag in her hand and takes another leap down onto terra firma and is off like the space shuttle; no explosions. Why wait for the baggage claim to mangle your bags when you've got an escape to make? She's up the stairs like a kamikaze homing pigeon, and he's right after her. Double takes as perfectly innocent travellers coming down the escalator get bumped aside by a fleeing paperhanger, a skip-tracer in pursuit — only he just wants to tell her goodbye. He wants to tell her he's going to join her. He might say he'll share the story if only she'd stay in it. He wants to get out of the way of the point of view. He's going to say he'll write home and say *Wish you were here* on a tacky postcard of the CN Tower. He'll say, *Let's go live in a revolving restaurant.* It's raining cats, buckets and Albanians outside, and he decides to tell her she'll catch her death of narrative; and if she decides to hang around he'll find something they can do together — cook, sew, or fly DC-3s into Peru loaded with bales of cheap detective mysteries; they'll make a mint. They'll switch off being pilots and co-pilots. No kidding, wait; they run past advertisements for fur coats, rum, and underwear; he's gaining. She's running up the stairs — or if not running, then walking extremely fast — with one pigskin bag (leave the others, they're not important), and he's walking just as quickly beside her. She says:

"You wanted the story all to yourself after all, didn't you? Well, you can have it. You can have all the credit too, and the ideas; and being pursued by mysterious men isn't as fun as it used to be in the forties. Everything's changed. You can have it; there's enough either on this credit card or that credit card to get me to Memphis — I'll go to Memphis and disappear into exotic chaos. I knew it when you got on the train. I smelled a rat. You can have the entire story: the dialogue, the italicized sections, the uppercase titles, everything. You think you're very uppercase, don't you? I'm going to leave this hemisphere of print altogether. You will not meet me again, not on paper, anyhow. It's not so far from Memphis to Honduras. The page will jump out of your hand; it will be blown away on a long, angelic wind — a print hurricane of solid wind and hard copy — to a port city and disappearance: missing characters."

Parting Scene

He stops her at the curb outside the massive Toronto train station, in a heavy November rain. A scene of parting; is it necessary? Water falling off of things: water falling off her hat, and drops forming on the strands of the little veil (now ripped in places), and water forming and gathering on the mink shoulders, water dropping and running around the edges of her ears and off her earrings, and the toes of her high heels, water falling from his hands and wrists as he draws together the edges of the fox collar, and water on their lips as they kiss.

She seems to be fading out; or dying. Erased. He draws her close as people run past them toward the taxis at the curb and then he reaches into her pocket for the train ticket; he thinks it might disintegrate in the rain. He wants to make sure it says St. Louis or Memphis, or Waco; wherever it is she's going. And he's not sure she's there at all, anyway. He's occupying the centre of the visual field so completely. He's sorry about this; confused. Is that her walking back into the gigantic station? Is that the noise of her thoughts; those trains? Is that the splashing of her footsteps and why did she leave? Why is he suddenly so hopelessly alone in the middle of the whole story? Our Hero. She is so wet she seems to have become counterfeit; or was it just him?

It was just him.

The End: King Street

It has become his story without any effort on his part; it was preconstructed. He feels suddenly overwhelmed with loss, and so he tries to light a cigarette and takes on water. He feels he has lost something (a story) forever that was of immense value, that would have made all the difference. He remembers what he thought he wanted was not what he really wanted, but who doesn't? You know. He wanted the end of her story.

He stands in the rain in his hat like a book cover and hears the vague report of big ships unloading somewhere at a harbour. There is always a lake or river near these big cities in the East, and dense smoke, as if the city had taken a direct hit sometime in the night. Women avoid his glance as they walk by; they always do. He feels he's missed it, but he can have it yet, if he hurries, if he makes his mind up *now*, right now. *How can you leave*, he asks her, or thinks he did, *and walk off like that, and leave and go to Memphis?* Now he knows what it is he wanted, and the discovering is like standing on the shore of near space and looking out beyond to the Horsehead Nebula, thinking, *If only I let go I'll float off into the hot and glowing rainbow of the interior, the Bengalese Crown jewels; and if only you would not get on the train south, and if only I could relocate you, and if only the noises of the ships' horns didn't keep sounding a narrative about something I almost had, and that I missed*; and he walks quickly into the train station.

The Beginning

She's been waiting for two hours and if he doesn't show up within another fifteen minutes, she's going on without him. The entire cargo of vintage *Black Mask* magazines, a complete set starting in 1920, was securely crated and waiting at the Frobisher Bay field. She put down the book she had been reading, a bit of fluff called *Sitting in the Club Car Drinking Rum and Karma-Kola: A Manual of Etiquette for Ladies Crossing Canada by Train*. She's waiting in a snack joint just west of the big high school gymnasium: a geodesic dome made to look like an igloo. Clever, these Canadians ... Can you imagine, looking just like an igloo! Wow. The local inhabitants must have been snowed. The snack joint was owned by an Italian who also ran a couple of taxis — Happy Bob's Polar Cab Company. Summertime in Frobisher Bay meant pack ice grinding down on several beached freighters out in the bay, and bad weather. If he didn't get here in fifteen minutes, she'd go without him.

"Waiting for somebody?"

"What were you doing, counting your brain cells?"

"Forget the snappy repartee; the guy's going to take off without us if we don't get loaded and go."

"Is this Dane really going to pop for the whole set? Is this all they have to read in Greenland?"

"He's an international dealer holed up in Nuuk."

"That sounds like you made it up."

"Smuggling rare books isn't as commonplace as it used to be."

Snappy repartee continues as they race in Happy Polar Bob's taxi for the airport. She and he kiss madly; he runs his hands through her short blonde hair. Air Greenland's Twin Otter spins its propellers. She tosses the book out the window; there'll be magazines on the plane — *The Cockpit*, maybe.

About the Author

Paulette Jiles is a poet, playwright, photojournalist and novelist who lives in San Antonio, Texas. Her poetry collection *Celestial Navigation* won The Governor-General's Award. She has also published *The Jesse James Poems* (Polestar), *Blackwater: New and Selected Poems* (Knopf), as well as *Song to the Rising Sun* (Polestar) and the non-fiction books *Cousins* (Knopf) and *North Spirit* (Doubleday). Her most recent novel is *Enemy Women* (HarperCollins), a bestseller in Canada and the United States, and winner of the prestigious Rogers Writer's Trust Fiction Prize.

ABOUT THE BOOK

Sitting in the Club Car Drinking Rum and Karma-Kola was typeset using
Filosofia, an interpretation of Bodoni designed by Suzanna Licko for
Emigre Inc. Though geometric in style, it incorporates such features as the
slightly bulging round serif endings which often appeared in printed samples
of Bodoni's work and reflect Bodoni's origins in letterpress technology.

The chapter title font is Ariston, a script font designed by Martin Wilke
in the 1920s for a then-popular German cigarette brand.